This book is dedicated to:

My son Terren Pray Jackson,
"Never Give Up."
&
The late Carol Cubbage Davis, and Janie Pierce
"Gone but Never Forgotten".

Text and illustrations Copyright © 2018 by Briana Pray
Printed in the U.S.A
Book Design and Graphic Art by James Hill
Edited by www.SheenaGates.com

I would like to thank the following, my Lord and Savior Jesus Christ. Without You I'm nothing. I would also like to give a special thank you to my mother, Sandra Pray-Cox, for all your love and support with everything I do in life. Thank you to my Pastor, Alice L. Martin, for the life changing messages. Thanks to all my family and friends for your guidance in this journey. I would especially like to acknowledge my previous dance schools LaCher-Tari Dance Studio and Progressive Center for Dance, where my dance foundation began.

Extra! Extra! Read all about it!
The Pirouette Center for Dance
will host It's annual show;
"A Little Night Dancing".

We are pleased to introduce, Sugga Bugga and her debut performance! The show is tomorrow night at 7pm sharp, at the Fine Arts Academy Theatre.

Dear Diary,

My big show is tomorrow!
This will be my first time dancing for a crowd.
I hope I do good! I'd better start practicing!

Signed,
an excited Sugga Bugga.

Sugga Bugga practiced and practiced until it was right to make sure she was ready for her big night!

Releve'!

Passe!

Sous Sous!

Tombe!

Developpe'!

Changement!

Sugga Bugga practiced her steps
and was ready for her performance.

"Showtime! Showtime!" Madame DelaTours clapped her hands and shouted. But Sugga Bugga was not ready. She was very nervous and afraid to hit the stage.

Dear Diary,

Today is the show, I don't know how it will go.
I practiced day and night, I practiced until it was right.
But my face is all hot and my muscles are tight.
Please tell me why? Am I nervous or am I shy?

Signed,
a confused Sugga Bugga

Madame DelaTours saw Sugga Bugga back stage and noticed she was sad. "Practice makes perfect and you have practiced with all of your might, you've come too far to have stage fright! So lift your head up and turn that frown upside down your dancing is sure to make the crowd go wow!" said Madame DelaTours.

"Welcome to the show, A Little Night Dancing! I am your host Lady Carol! Sit back and relax for a night of grace and style that is sure to make you smile. Put your hands together and get on your feet because this first dance is a real treat!" Lady Carol said as she greeted the audience.

Sugga Bugga heard Madame DelaTours say
"Get into your spots! Curtains! Que the lights!
Music! Dancers! Go" But Sugga Bugga's legs
said "NO!" Sugga Bugga had stage fright
while standing in the spotlight.

The music played while the dancers jumped from leg to leg. Sugga Bugga opened her eyes to join the dancers side by side. Kick! Jump! Stomp! And Bump! Sugga Bugga went down. Thump! Clump Clump!

"AHHHHH!!!"
Sugga Bugga cried.

Sugga Bugga's fears came true,
she forgot her steps, and the performance was a
wreck. Sugga Bugga ran off of the stage.

Dear Diary,

I messed up bad and now I'm sad.
I bet you Mom and Dad will be very mad!!

Signed,
an embarrassed Sugga Bugga

Another dancer, Jae P was waiting for her turn
to dance when she saw Sugga Bugga. "Hi, what's
your name?" she said. "My name is Sugga Bugga."
"What's wrong, why do you look so sad?" Jae P asked.
"I messed up my dance. I'm really embarrassed."
said Sugga Bugga

Jae P told Sugga Bugga "Performing can be very scary,
it might make you feel funny on the inside and you
might cry on the outside. But dancing in front of
people makes them happy because you're showing
them talents that God gave you. So lift your head up
and put on a smile, the crowd is waiting for you to make
them say Wow!"

Dear Diary,

I met a new friend named Jae P. She wasn't afraid to dance on stage. She shared some kind words to help me along and I'm glad to say my stage fright is gone!

Signed,
a hopeful Sugga Bugga

Sugga Bugga wiped her tears and put on a smile before she went back on stage.

Sugga Bugga remembered what Jae P said and when she stepped out she heard a voice from the crowd say, "Dance Sugga Bugga, you can do it!"

Sugga Bugga knew the voice, it was Momma Sugga and Papa Sugga too! So she lifted her head, and began to dance. She danced and danced just like she practiced. And the crowd said "Wow!"

"YAAAAAAY!"

the crowd cheered.

Dear Diary,

I conquered my fears of stage fright and danced well tonight! I can't wait until the next show I know it will be such a delight!

Love ,
Sugga Bugga

THE END!

Dear Diary,

_____

_____

_____

_____

_____

_____

_____

_____

_____

_____

_____

_____

_____

Love,

_____

Dear Diary,

_____

_____

_____

_____

_____

_____

_____

_____

_____

_____

_____

_____

_____

_____

Love,

_____

Dear Diary,

_____
_____
_____
_____
_____
_____
_____
_____
_____
_____
_____
_____
_____
_____
_____

Love,

_____

Dear Diary,

_____
_____
_____
_____
_____
_____
_____
_____
_____
_____
_____
_____
_____
_____
_____

Love,

_____

In the book Stage Fright, Sugga Bugga is very nervous to dance on stage. She is very familiar with practicing until she gets better, but being nervous made her forget her dance during the show. If you noticed at the end of the book, Sugga Bugga did much better with her second dance which wasn't ballet. Sometimes we find there are other things that we are just better at. When we find what works best for us, that's when it's time to focus and invest in that talent.

Note to Students:

There are many things that make us nervous in life. Being in front of people and sharing something personal such as a special talent is sure to make your nerves jump. Here are some ways that could help calm your nerves down.

Recognize It - When you have that feeling of butterflies in your stomach or negative thoughts racing in your head. Acknowledge your fears, close your eyes and take a deep breath. Knowing is half the battle.

Accept It- When you accept that you are nervous, pray for strength to get you through your nervous feelings. You could also find a person that you are comfortable with talking to that could help boost your confidence up.

Visualize It- Think about your goals and what you want to achieve. Then think about the reward that comes with achieving your goals. This should give you a lot of motivation to push through the nervous feelings and receive the blessing of your goals.

Note to Parents & Teachers,

As you know, children get nervous when they have to perform or do something in front of a big crowd. Helping children overcome their fears by giving them inspiring and positive words will help them with their fears. However, inspiring words are good, but an inspiring walk is much better. If your actions line up with your inspiring words, children will overcome their fears and become extraordinary. Always remember that you are their first role model.

BIO

Briana Pray is from Philadelphia, Pa. and started her dance career at the age of 5 under the instruction of Cheryl G. Jenkins at LaCher-Tari Dance Studio. During her stay at La Cher-Tari Dance School, Briana studied ballet, tap, jazz, hip-hop and African dance. In 1994, Briana joined the Progressive Center for Dance Studio under the direction of the late Carol Cubbage Davis. At PCD, Briana was introduced to modern dance, along with some techniques in Dunham and Graham.

Briana continues to share her talents with others as a traveling dance instructor at Leaders and Legends Performing Arts Center and Ms. Carol's Center for Dance (formerly known as Progressive Center for Dance). Briana lives in Philadelphia, Pa. with her son who is her entire world.